Turtle People

Turtle People

Brenda Z. Guiberson

ATHENEUM   1990   NEW YORK

COLLIER MACMILLAN CANADA
Toronto
MAXWELL MACMILLAN INTERNATIONAL PUBLISHING GROUP
New York   Oxford   Singapore   Sydney

Atheneum
Macmillan Publishing Company
866 Third Avenue, New York, NY 10022

Collier Macmillan Canada, Inc.
1200 Eglinton Avenue East
Suite 200
Don Mills, Ontario M3C 3N1

First Edition
Printed in the United States of America
Designed by Kimberly M. Hauck
10 9 8 7 6 5 4 3 2 1

Library of Congress Cataloging-in-Publication Data
Guiberson, Brenda Z.
Turtle People/Brenda Z. Guiberson.—1st ed. p. cm.
Summary: Depressed by the continuing absence of his beloved father
and the distant behavior of his mother, eleven-year-old Richie
retreats to a remote island near his Washington State home and finds
a great archeological mystery.
ISBN 0–689–31647–X
[1. Archaeology—Fiction. 2. Fathers and sons—Fiction.
3. Family problems—Fiction. 4. Washington (State)—Fiction.]
I. Title.
PZ7.G93833Tu 1990 [Fic]—dc20
90–388 CIP AC

For Jason, and for Bill

Turtle People

THE PEAR FARM IS GREEN BECAUSE WE IRRIGATE IT, but the rest of the land around here is mostly sand, and sagebrush, and flat. When I wanted to get out of the way last summer, I could. It was easy. Eastern Washington is full of wide open spaces.

The best place I found was the Snake River, not too far and not too close. I'd run there, across the desert, until sweat dripped down my face and dust covered the sweat. Then I'd dive in deep. Hot to cold, dusty to clean, there was nothing else like it.

It made me feel like something had changed, even though nothing really had.

Dad was still gone, and Mom was hardly talking to anybody. Mostly she left notes all over the house. REMEMBER SUNSCREEN. LOVE, MOM. REMOVE YOUR SHOES HERE. LOVE, MOM. MAKE NEW ICE CUBES. LOVE, MOM.

Staying around the house—empty of adults and full of yellow memos—was impossible. My little sister called the notes momos. "What did Mom say in this momo?" she'd ask. "What does she want you to do now, Richie?" Ellen can't read much yet so she usually got notes with pictures on them. Every morning, there was a picture of a toothbrush for her on the kitchen table.

"Why doesn't she just come out and eat breakfast with us?" Ellen would say. And then she'd stomp into the bathroom and turn the water on full blast.

"See, I'm brushing my teeth," she yelled out. But usually she wasn't. Mostly she sat on the edge of the bathtub and picked at her toenails.

And Mom would clean the house, vacuum here, scour there, scrub, wash, rinse.

The only way to escape all this was to dive into the river and stay out there, somewhere.

Usually I swam out to the island. It was a perfect place, warm and sandy, protected by rushing water on all sides. It reminded me of all the places my father had taken me—our "expeditions to the past," he called them.

We used to poke around the dunes, out in the desert, and sift hot sand, looking for arrowheads and spear points and the rocks used by Indians to weigh down fishing nets. Once in a while, we found something left behind hundreds, maybe thousands, of years ago.

Dad loved the expeditions. Whenever he could take time from the pear trees, we went. When we found an artifact, he'd jump around yelling, "Eureka, we've found it! How many does that make?"

I always wanted to know something about what we found, but Dad never cared too much. He was mainly interested in numbers. If you had two arrowheads, four would be better, sixteen would be better yet. "Keep looking, Richie," he'd say. He was always looking for more, more, more.

Mom didn't like us to go, but we went anyway. And she didn't like the things that we found, but we found them anyway. "You're bringing more dust into the house," she'd say. It made me feel like I was in the middle, where I didn't want to be.

After Dad left, I went on expeditions to the island, but it wasn't the same. I just searched through the sand until my problems seemed far away. I never really expected to find anything because my concentration was gone. You have to pay attention to tell one gray rock from the gray sand, from another gray rock.

One day, after Dad had been gone for weeks and weeks, I was out on the island, trying to forget a totally unfair note from my mother. NO PAPER ROUTE. REMEMBER DINNER. LOVE, MOM.

I wanted to be a sub for Chad Henderson (Henny, I call him) when he needed help. Henny knows a lot about almost everything. On my first day of school here, a year ago last spring, he came right up to me and said, "Hi, we're doing history reports. You should be my partner so you can start things off with a good grade."

Everyone else was doing Columbus, or the Pilgrims, but we did the Lewis and Clark Expedition. I found out a few things in the encyclopedia and wrote them up. But Henny came up with so much information that, all of a sudden, Lewis and Clark started to seem like real people to me. I knew they had gotten cactus stickers in their feet and had a hard time with fleas and mosquitoes. And neither one of them could spell very well.

So Henny and I became great friends, and when he needed something, naturally I was the guy to help out. The only problem was his newspapers had to be delivered during the "dinner hour." Nothing was allowed to interrupt the "dinner hour" in our family. I missed out on more things in life because of this rule. Everyone had to be home for our family time when we chewed and argued together.

When there were four of us, Mom said we had to be home for dinner because that's what Dad wanted. But after he left, we still had to be home, *always*. And he was home, *never*.

After Dad left, Ellen spent most of her time telling me what to do, when she could find me. "Now *Richie*," she yelled, loud and clear. "Don't *do* that."

Sometimes she sounded like Mom, trying to get Dad to be different.

I liked Dad just the way he was, except that he wasn't home.

Anyway, that's why I was poking around on the island, trying not to think about all this stuff. I had the place to myself, which was just fine. I was trying to forget all about that momo on the paper route and I certainly didn't feel like talking to anyone, about anything.

The people at one of the dams must have been up to something because the waterline was very, very low. I found two obsidian chips and one of petrified wood right away, without even looking, with no concentration going on at all.

The chips were left by Indians hitting rocks together to make arrowheads. Henny and I had found that out at the Sacajawea Museum. For hundreds of years, Indians walked right across my island. They caught salmon there and smoked it. They lived in mat houses and crossed the river in handmade canoes. You knew they'd been there because they left things behind.

As soon as I found the chips, I tried to imagine what the people were like who made them. It was like making a composite sketch for the police. Did they wear deerskin robes? Any eagle feathers in their hair? What about huckleberry stains on their moccasins? One papoose, or two?

It made me feel like part of an adventure. I felt the same way about the Lewis and Clark Expedition. Meriwether Lewis and William Clark came down the Snake River, right past my island. Were they hungry? Were they happy to see the Columbia River? Sacajawea and her baby, Jean-Baptiste—only Lewis and Clark called him Pomp—were there too. That Pomp was a lucky little guy. His parents went on a trip together, and he got to come along, riding on his mother's back the whole way.

My mother used to carry Ellen around in a front sack. It was red and white and had a little bib that snapped on by the baby's head. She didn't have one of those for me, but there are lots of pictures of us in the rocking chair.

After I found the chips, I really started to notice how different the island looked. I could walk way down into places I'd never been, down below the usual waterline. Small, thirsty plants were getting crusty in the sun, and muddy banks made a big ring around the island.

I walked across some slippery rocks and sloshed through an area of rotting green algae. I held my nose. The strong smell of slimy goo was everywhere.

I poked my toes into a dimple in some wet, squishy sand, just the kind Ellen would like for mud pies. And one of the kinds my mother did not like at all. I wondered how long the sand had been covered with water. Was this an ancient spot, untouched by anything but fish for hundreds of years? It was a very exciting thought, that's for sure.

I scooped up a big glob of the stuff with my toes and sloshed it around. I was getting used to the smell, so I did it again, and again, and again.

It was such a mindless activity. I was on my way to forgetting the note, the paper route, and Dad's empty chair. I was on my way to forgetting how unhappy I really was.

What I didn't know was that the next scoop of sand would have nothing to do with forgetting. The next scoop was enough to jolt me right out of a peaceful routine and into some real excitement. It was the next scoop that led to the Great Discovery.

2

I SAW A CURVED LINE IN THE SAND AND FELT IT WITH
my toes. Something big and solid was under there.
I thought it might be a mortar and pestle like my
dad had found, but I secretly hoped that it would
be something even more terrific.

I wasn't in a big hurry to find out because I
didn't want to be disappointed. Usually I think
something's going to be big and then it turns out
to be little. Or maybe medium, at the most.

Like when we bought the pear farm. Dad said it
would be just the thing to fix up our family. He

could stay home all the time and help Mom and life would be zippety-doo-dah. Ha!

Three of us loved the farm, but Mom did not. "Don't you like pears, Mom?" said Ellen.

"Of course I do," she said. "That's not the point."

My mother didn't like the dust, or the heat, or the lack of neighbors. She used to be the kind of person who liked all sorts of things and got others interested in them too. But now she didn't seem to like anything.

The only thing she could fix was the dust. Mom spent most of her time cleaning the house. "How anyone could live out here without two good vacuums is beyond me," she told my dad every time the wind blew. "It doesn't help to close the windows. It comes in anyway."

"But why do you need two?" Dad had asked.

"You're the one who wanted a two-story house," said Mom. "I won't carry a big vacuum up and down these stairs." Before the year was out, we actually had three: one for the upstairs, one for downstairs, and a little one for the stairway in between.

Mom and Dad argued about things a lot, which was terrible. But after a while, they hardly talked at all, and that seemed much worse.

That's when Dad and I started training Blueboy to retrieve things from the water. Blueboy is our big, friendly, jump-up-on-you dog. He's a black Lab. Mom named him after a famous painting. She named me Richard Adams Burroughby after the two Adamses who were presidents of the United States. This is a name that is supposed to make me famous. It's made me famous, all right. I know four kids in the sixth grade, and they all call me Richie.

The Indians were lucky. They could have any name they wanted, and then change it later if they liked. I wouldn't mind being called Swims Like A Fish for a while.

Blueboy probably should have been named Runs After Anything. He was hard to train. He went into the water when he felt like it and then he shook all over us when he got out. So we stayed away from the water and tried to teach him to "sit" and "stay."

Blueboy did not seem interested. He usually took off to chase jackrabbits in the desert. And then we could hardly get him to come back.

One day Dad jogged all through the pear or-chard to retrieve Blueboy, and that's when he found the mortar and pestle, near a rabbit hole. "Eureka!" he shouted to me. "Come see this. Just look. It's the tools the Indians used for grinding."

That was the beginning of our "expeditions into the past." We left Blueboy at home and did some serious looking. Dad looked even when he was out checking the pears. We didn't find much, but that didn't mean that we never would.

"Let's go after dinner," Dad would say. "This is going to be the trip when we really find something. I can just feel it."

Then one time, Mom and Dad talked loud and long into the night. The next morning, Dad was gone. Gone! He had packed up a suitcase and left.

Mom cried all morning and it was a long time before she told us anything. "Lots of things are wrong," she said. "And one of the worst is that we aren't getting a good pear crop this year."

"But why did Dad leave?" said Ellen.

"Dad went to Seattle to earn some extra money. He wasn't sure what he'd do, but said we could reach him at Uncle Doug's."

"Uncle Doug is never home," said Ellen. "He's always going someplace."

"Well," said Mom. "He has an answering machine."

A machine! Dad expected us to call him at a machine? I was so angry I didn't say anything. Dad was off on some new expedition, and he had left me behind.

Sometimes I thought that if only I could find *the most terrific artifact,* then Dad would come back, right away, to see it. At least I hoped he would. But we hadn't heard from him in a long time. He had been gone so many weeks that I didn't know if he was exactly the same anymore.

So that day out on the island, when I was slowly swishing things around with my feet, I wasn't sure if I wanted to find anything that good or not. What if I found it and then Dad didn't come back? Why couldn't he come back, anyway?

The dimple I was poking at with my feet became a hole with a little blip at one end. Interesting, very interesting. I gazed at a sea gull in the sky so I wouldn't get too excited. Did I want to keep looking or not?

I glanced back at the hole. It was still there. Swish, swish. Soon a rim showed. Swish, then the sides. Swish, swish, swish. Then everything, even the little feet on the bottom.

I couldn't believe my luck. Out of all that muck and slime came something absolutely beautiful. I splashed it to rinse off some of the sand and just stood there with my mouth hanging open. If the island had a phone booth, I'd have called Dad and shouted, "Eureka, I've found it." And he'd know exactly what that meant.

It's amazing what you can find when you are

not even looking. Not even sure you want to look. But there it was, a carved stone bowl about the size of a football, just waiting to be held in my arms. I picked it up carefully, gently, with total respect. I had never seen anything like it at the Sacajawea Museum. I figured it had to be rare. It was probably very, very rare.

The bowl had a small head at one end, a flat ridge at the other, and four round feet at the bottom. Lots of fancy designs were carved along the sides. It looked like a turtle. Indians usually chose eagles, or wolves, or bears.

Well, I liked the idea that someone chose a turtle. I like turtles. They take care of themselves and don't bother anybody. And boy, can they swim. The Indians must have had lots of good reasons for choosing a turtle.

I figured the people who lived out on this island loved turtles. Their mat houses were probably shaped like turtle shells. It would be easy to carve a canoe into a turtle shape. Of course, those things couldn't still be around because the materials would have rotted away.

But I had found a turtle carved in *stone*. It had to be lasting evidence of a turtle culture. Evidence of a whole tribe of Turtle People living on that island, imitating a peaceful water creature that eats fish and basks in the sun and stays out of everybody's way.

I could practically smell the red salmon cooking over their fire. Did they like sturgeon? Maybe they kept a carved turtle in a wooden box and took it out only for ceremonies and feasts. Over by the sage would be a good place for the drummer, tapping on something shaped like a turtle.

New ideas about the Turtle People kept popping into my head. I took a piece of driftwood and pushed aside the wet sand to make a small scale map of how the place must have looked. I broke off pieces of tall grass and wove them into miniature mat houses. Then I wove some little people and poked them into the sand.

Weaving. That's something my mom taught me, back in the days when she led our Cub Scout troop. But she hasn't taught me anything new in a long time.

The little village was starting to look pretty good. I made a place for a campfire and moved some of the people over to it. I could imagine them talking about turtles. They probably kept turtles as pets.

I found some teeny rounded river rocks to be the turtles. Then I added one more woven figure. It was the hardest one because I tried to make him sitting down. I had to pack sand around to keep him from falling over. Then I made a big sand mound and put the turtle bowl on top.

The side of the bowl had lots of lines, like some kind of writing. When Lewis and Clark came through, the Indians had no written language. They passed along information through tales and legends. But maybe thousands of years ago there was a written language. And that was it, right on the bowl. I had to know what those lines meant. They had to be clues about the people who left it behind. They could be important messages.

I might be important if I could just figure it all out.

My mind was full of questions and I wished someone were there who could answer them. But the biggest question was this: How was I going to swim back to shore with a stone bowl in one hand? I was a strong swimmer, but this was a big bowl. There was no way the two of us could side-stroke together across the Snake.

My only choice was to hide the bowl and come back later with a boat or something. What a choice. What if someone came? What if they noticed freshly turned earth? They would look, that's what they'd do. Anyone who hung out around the river knew that there were things to be found.

I had to be tricky and hide the bowl in a spot

where no one would look. I took the bowl to the middle of the island, where it was drier and covered with prickly plants and swarming with caddis flies.

I dug near an anthill, full of red stinging ants. It seemed like a good way to keep people away. I could hardly wait to get out of there myself.

I was so worried that I'd lose the Great Discovery. The ants were good, but not enough. Then I remembered that when Lewis and Clark stored things in the ground they always made sure the spot did not look freshly dug. I covered the area with a pile of tumbleweeds for camouflage and topped this off with handfuls of dirt.

It made a lot of dust, but when everything settled, it was perfect. The bowl was buried without a trace.

I breathed in deeply and felt better than I had for weeks. I couldn't believe that, almost by accident, I'd found the best artifact ever.

I had touched history, maybe even prehistory. If things went as expected, I could become an important part of history myself. Richard Adams Burroughby, top-notch archaeologist, discoverer of the Turtle Phase of the lower Snake River.

And maybe, just maybe, the discoverer of something so exciting that Dad would want to come back and see it for himself.

3

I$_T$ WAS MIDAFTERNOON WHEN I SWAM OFF THE IS-
land. I had to pick up my things at Henny's before
I went home. I always left my bike and shirt at his
house so that I could jog the rest of the way to the
river. By the time I jogged back, I was hot and
sweaty and dusty again. The river seemed so far
away when I wasn't in it.

"Hey, Henny," I called when I saw him on the
porch. "How come you're not in the house admir-
ing your baseball cards?"

"Gotta fold the newspapers," he said. "I don't
know how I'll deliver them today. It's a hundred

18

and two right here in the shade. You should keep out of that sun. With your red hair, you'll have a zillion freckles before you're twelve."

"Forget the heat, Henny," I said. "In a few weeks, I can hire someone to deliver the papers for you."

"How do you plan to do that?" said Henny. "You haven't made a dime all summer. In fact, it's surprising you don't look wrinkled and pruny with all that swimming you do."

"Swimming pays off," I said. "I just made the Great Discovery of my life."

"*You* met a girl?" said Henny. "I thought you were avoiding people out on your island."

"Henny!" I said. "This has nothing to do with girls." Then I told him all about the bowl and how wonderful it was.

"Way to be," he said. "You're putting some real life into our summer. Where is it?"

I checked to make sure no one was around and then, in a whispering voice, I told him everything. I trusted Henny completely. He liked everything I liked except for one thing—he couldn't swim.

I've tried to teach him but we never even got to the jellyfish float. He doesn't like anything athletic, unless you consider baseball cards athletic. On the other hand, Henny has a photographic memory. Once he knows something, he never forgets. He told me once that turtles have been around for 150 million years. Now, how many friends know some useful fact like that?

However, Henny knew more about the Snake River than he ever needed to know. "Water from the Rocky Mountains is very cold," he said, when I tried to get him in to swim. "The current moves too fast and dumps you right into the mighty Columbia." He shivered and pulled his toes back from the edge of the water. "And this is somebody's home," he said, with his arms out like the conductor of an orchestra. "Think of all the fish and tiny creatures that live in there and didn't give us an invitation. Leave this water for irrigation and electrical power. I'm not getting in."

Henny likes to give long speeches like that. I told him we'd try the pool in Pasco. No current, no algae, and you can see the bottom. Getting in pool water is a real sacrifice for me. One hour in that chlorinated water and I cry like a baby. Allergies! Good thing I'm not allergic to dust.

"You need a boat," said Henny. "Ask your mom if you can use the boat."

"Out of the question," I said. "The boat is all polished up and for sale in front of our house. Besides I don't think she'd like it if she knew I went out there."

"Your mother doesn't know you've spent all

summer languishing on a river island? Without sunscreen?" Henny covered his eyes and tried to look horrified.

"She doesn't keep track of things like she used to. As long as I don't get the house dirty and show up for the 'dinner hour,' she thinks everything is okay. She even wrote me a momo once: THANKS FOR KEEPING YOUR ROOM CLEAN. LOVE, MOM."

"Well, your room is clean because you're never in it. But that doesn't solve the problem of a boat. Where is a good boat when you need one?" Henny plopped down on the porch glider and squinted his eyes. That's what he does when he searches his photographic memory.

"There's Gil," he said. Gil is an interesting old man that we talk to at Sacajawea Park. He used to collect things for the museum.

"He gets more excited about artifacts than Ellen does at an Easter-egg hunt," I said. "He reads a lot too. Maybe he could tell me more about the bowl."

"The bowl sounds unusual," said Henny. "I'm dying to get some real facts on that thing."

"Well, I already know that I discovered a lost tribe of Turtle People. I don't know what happened to them, but they lived on that island a long time ago."

"Hold on," said Henny. "Ho-o-o-ld on. It's true that tribes of Indians have died out. The Palouse, and the Mandans, and there's only one Wanapum left."

"Only one Wanapum left? *Only one?* When Lewis and Clark came through here, there were over two thousand."

"Well, now there's only one," said Henny. "I met him up at Wanapum Dam."

I dropped my head and swallowed real hard. That was just about the saddest thing I'd ever heard. And I could hardly bear the thought that, at some time, there had been only one last Turtle Person.

"I've never heard of any Turtle People," said Henny. "Who are you talking about?"

"Well, they're gone now," I said. "But they were people who looked to the turtle for a way of life. A good way of life, I might add."

And then my mind flashed ahead to the day when they would award a great medal and dedicate a museum to me, Richard Adams Burroughby. Maybe my mother was right and I would be famous. And Dad would come back to watch them put the medal around my neck.

"First thing tomorrow," I said, "let's ride our bikes to the park and find Gil. It's time to bring back the turtle bowl."

"It's about time," said Henny, "that you wanted to do something besides take a swim."

ELLEN CAME STORMING IN THE NEXT MORNING, RIGHT
in the middle of a great dream I was having about
the Turtle People.

"Wake up, Richie!" shouted Ellen. "Come on.
Get out of that bed."

"Ellen," I groaned. "You're ruining a good
dream. Now I've forgotten it completely."

"Mom says you dream too much," said Ellen.
"Hurry up. This is a three-two-one day."

"Wait a minute," I said. "This is summer. Au-
gust. How could it be a three-two-one day?"

On school days, Mom had a system. Five minutes to dress, ten minutes for breakfast, and five minutes for hair, teeth, and everything else. That would be a five-ten-five day, our usual.

Sometimes we overslept and then we had a three-two-one day. This meant "put on the first thing you see and grab a piece of fruit on the way out." I do not like three-two-one days ever, but especially not when I have plans of my own.

"Mom says we have to see the dentist at eight-thirty," said Ellen. "She just remembered. I'm going to spend the whole three-two-one on my teeth."

"Forget it," I said. "There's no way you can clean those teeth now. Just leave some toothpaste for me."

Oh rats, I thought as I slipped on my swim trunks and T-shirt. I didn't need the interruption, not with all the important things I had to do.

It had been a hard night for sleeping. All I could think about was the people who carved that stone into a turtle.

Once, in Cub Scouts, Mom tried to show us how to whittle. We took some soft balsa wood and tried to make a bear. Our bears were too thin, and crooked. We either made the snout too long, or too short. Mom said we really had to know what something looked like before we could carve it well.

So I knew that someone had studied turtles, a lot of turtles, to make one that looked so good. And the stone had a smooth surface with curved shapes and designs. For someone to make it, in stone no less, would take lots of time, and lots of patience.

I could imagine a great chief gathering his tribe into a long mat house with fresh sand sprinkled on the floor. And in the middle would be a turtle, several turtles actually, to inspire the Turtle People to lead slow, peaceful lives. They would know all about time and patience. They probably worked together as families, making fancy things in no real hurry.

If an enemy came, they could just hide in the murky water or cover up in the sand. Probably they didn't even have enemies.

I wanted to know about their language, their culture, everything. Maybe they had an answer for me.

But first I had to go to the dentist. Double rats!

"Oh, dear," said Mom when I came downstairs. "You aren't going to wear that to the dentist's office, are you? Well, there's no time to change. Let's go."

"Mom," I said. "Good morning. How are you doing? Listen, could I go to the dentist later? Important things to do today."

Mom wearily pointed to the yellow paper on the table that announced, THIS IS A 3-2-1 DAY, in bright red crayon.

"Does that mean no, Mom?" I said. "Why don't you just say so?"

Mom shrugged her shoulders and looked at me sadly. "I'm sorry. You'll have to go," she said. "I can't change the appointment now."

I picked up a napkin and scribbled a reply. SO LET'S GET MOVING. And we did, without even time for a piece of fruit.

At Dr. Dory's office, Ellen cried and fussed and had perfect teeth. I sat quietly through the whole exam and he found two cavities, my first. I was shocked!

Mom was embarrassed. She pointed to the chart Dr. Dory keeps of all the kids who have perfect teeth. "Now you won't get to be in the Great Teeth Club," she said. "Maybe you need to brush longer. Ellen seems to spend more time at it than you."

I looked up at the bright, curved light over my head and thought about the sun shining on the even-tempered Turtle People. They would never get upset over teeth, such a small part of the big scheme of things.

But Mom was very upset. "You just don't care about things," she said, too loudly, with too much color in her cheeks. Then suddenly she stopped herself, pulled herself in, like a turtle backing into a shell. She took a quick breath and brushed back her hair.

I was shocked all over again. My own mother, acting like a turtle. I wondered how the Turtle People handled things when they got upset. If you looked to the turtle for an answer, it seemed like they would do just what Mom did. Retreat. What kind of an answer was that?

Maybe crawling into a shell would work if you weren't angry anymore. But Mom was still angry. I could feel it. It was like I'd done something awful, or someone had done something awful. It was a feeling I'd had all summer.

"Now, now," said Dr. Dory. "We'll fix him up in no time. Two half-hour appointments should do it." Then he peered through his glasses and lifted my chin. "We'll be watching to see if there is room for those new molars," he said. "Richie may need braces soon."

Mom didn't say anything. She was back where no one could reach her. Did she even hear him?

Well, I heard. Braces! They'd have to find me first. I hoped Dr. Dory couldn't swim. I already knew that my mother had never been in anything deeper or colder than bathtub water.

After the dentist, I asked Mom to drop me off at

Henny's. She'd never been there before and started asking questions. "Henny?" she said. "What kind of name is that? What does his father do, dear? I hope they don't let you eat junk food."

I jumped out of the car. "Bye, Mom," I said. "I have to go."

Ellen shouted out after me, "You shouldn't be running with thongs on your feet."

I ran up to Henny, who was putting baseball rookie cards into sheets with plastic pockets. "Boy, are you late," he said. "Where have you been?"

"I had to go to the dentist. What are you doing to those cards?"

"This is the best way to protect them," he said. "If you get any grease marks or bends in the cardboard, they are no longer in mint condition. They won't be worth as much money when you go to cash in your investment."

Henny thinks of baseball cards as the way to pay for college. I think of them as a way to learn statistics on my favorite players. I read the backs of the cards all the time. Henny reads the price guides like he was following the stock market. He told me that my 1985 Roger Clemens was worth $10.00. I have three of them. That's why I know that I can trust Henny. He didn't have to tell me that. He could have just traded me with a card that was worth a nickel. I thought they were all worth the price of a pack of gum.

"When you didn't show up," said Henny, "I decided to organize these Donruss rookies. You *are* saving all of your rookie cards, Richie? They're the ones that really go up in value."

"Have you ever seen a rookie who wore braces?" I said. "The dentist just said I might have to get them. And he found two cavities. My mouth will be full of metal."

"More problems?" said Henny. "I hope this doesn't mean you are going to leave me standing here while you take a swim."

"Nope," I said. "We've got better things to do. So let's do them."

5

HENNY PUT THE CARDS AWAY AND GOT OUT HIS BIKE. It's a brand-new shiny BMX Diamondback, loaded with extra gadgets that Henny buys with his newspaper money. Henny started to check things over—cables, speedometer, tire pressure, mirror adjustment—and then he sprayed the chain with WD 40. He always does this, even if he's going two blocks to the grocery.

"Almost ready," he said, when I thought he was all done. "I'm going to fill the water bottle and throw a bag of dried fruit into the seat pack." Then he made one more trip for a bandage, just in case.

30

When we finally got going, it was the hottest part of the day. I didn't want to know how hot it was, but I knew Henny was going to tell me.

"Did you check the thermometer?" he called up to me at the first intersection. "A hundred and five in the shade. It's hot enough to uncurl your hair. We'll die of heat exhaustion out here on the highway. Can't we go in something air-conditioned?"

Henny never does anything without a few complaints. He has terrible things to say about trumpet lessons but he likes to play the trumpet. And then there are book reports. Henny reads the long, nonfiction books, the Yellow Pages, everything. Just don't ask him to write up a report, because he will complain about it forever, and then turn in thirty pages.

"There's no way I'm going to ride across that thing," said Henny when we got to the bridge. "Not with all those big farm trucks whooshing past."

"Well, then, let's get off and walk," I said. It's a very narrow bridge. They were building a new one right next to it. It didn't look much wider.

"Henny," I called up. "Did the bridge crew ever find any artifacts when they started to dig around here?"

Henny glared back at me. "This is no place for a chitchat," he said. Then he looked straight ahead and nervously walked across.

On the other side, he answered my question. "I never heard of anything," he said. "But a man from Spokane once predicted that someday, someone would discover a Viking buried around here. He's sure the burial will have a written record of a battle between the Vikings and the Indians in A.D. 1010. Did your bowl have any Vikings on it?"

"Be serious," I said. "It's a turtle bowl, made by Turtle People, and that's all."

"I am serious," said Henny. "There's supposed to be an Indian legend that supports this Viking theory. Know of any legends to support the Turtle People?"

"There probably *is* one," I said. "Grandfathers, storytellers, dreamers, dancers, they all must have had tales to tell about the Turtle People. It was just so long ago, maybe the stories have been forgotten."

"Well, it's an interesting theory," said Henny. "I always like to learn something new."

"Maybe Gil can give us some details," I said. "He knows all about these things. Hop back on your bike and let's go."

"We still have a two-mile ride to the park," said Henny. "Aren't there any shortcuts?"

"We don't want to get off the main road," I said. "There's too many tack weeds out there."

"Those stickers are worse than real tacks," said Henny. "Maybe we should leave our bikes and walk. I don't want to take any chances."

That's the trouble with having such a nice bike, with so many terrific gadgets. Henny doesn't like to ride unless conditions are ideal, like maybe around a newly paved parking lot.

"Henny," I said. "It's definitely time for us to move on. Your inner tubes will be safe if you just stay on the highway. Besides, it will be cooler with a breeze blowing in your face."

Henny got back on his bike and slowly pedaled it up to a speed past wobbly but short of smooth and comfortable. "This is not a breeze," he called up to me. "This is hot air being forced up my nostrils. This is hot air drying out my already parched throat. Water. I need water."

I hated to stop again, but I stopped. Henny got out the water bottle and we had some. It was unrefreshingly warm and tasted like moldy garden hose. The Indians drank water from woven baskets or skin bags. Most likely a great improvement over a red plastic bottle.

Another wobble, another swerve, and we got going again. Henny was in front this time and I saw him check his compass. "Too bad we have to head this way," he shouted, pointing across the highway. "Right into the sun."

We made our turn onto the side road. It was much quieter away from the traffic, easier to talk.

"When did the Indians get horses around here?" I asked.

"Not until about 1730. Why?"

"Well, I was just wondering how the Indians got around. Of course, the Turtle People didn't have to worry about that. They just stayed out on the island all the time."

"They couldn't do that *all* the time," said Henny. "Sometimes they'd have to go hunting, or look for berries or roots."

"Well, how could they ever learn that from a turtle?"

"Maybe you're only partly right, Richie. Maybe they were Turtle–Coyote–Frog–Grizzly-Bear People."

"Maybe not," I said, and picked up the speed a bit.

"Slow down, Richard," yelled Henny, so I did. Henny rode up next to me and complained about bike grease and saddle sores. He mentioned all the different parts of his body that were getting sunburned and overworked.

I ignored him. He's my friend and it was okay

if he wanted to talk, just as long as he kept pedaling. I searched the desert for signs of Turtle People, in case they ever had come off the island. I looked for turtle petroglyphs carved into rocks, or stone tools with turtle handles. I didn't see anything.

Finally we rode into the shady park where the Snake flows into the Columbia River. Henny was a hot, grouchy, dripping mess. "Boy," he said, "I thought we'd never get off these bikes again."

"We could cool off with a quick swim," I said. But Henny made a face that said we couldn't.

We had another drink of water and Henny lifted up the flap of his seat pack. The plastic bag inside was hot and steamy and it stuck to the dried fruit in one gooey mess. "What a waste," said Henny, and he threw the whole bag away.

Then we looked for Gil. That's what we had come to do.

Henry and I walked all through the museum looking for him. We looked on the artifact side, and the Lewis and Clark side, but Gil wasn't there.

We looked for him on the dock and up and down the beach. Then we asked the ranger, but she hadn't seen him. The woman who sells nachos told us the same thing.

"What if he doesn't come today?" groaned Henny. "Does that mean we have to ride out here again tomorrow?"

"We have to do whatever it takes."

Henny groaned again, and again. "Come on," he said. "We're making our best effort to find him *today.*"

We finally spotted Gil in the stone gazebo, his white hair pasted to his forehead with sweat.

He was wearing loafers and soft cotton clothes. He always looks like he is just one step away from going to bed. And there he was, sound asleep and snoring. He sounded like a bubble machine.

"Hey, Gil," said Henny. "Wake up. We've got important news about artifacts. *Artifacts, Gil. Wake up!*"

Gil snorted. "I wasn't asleep," he said. "Just resting my eyes. Now what's this about artifacts?"

He stretched and yawned. "Oh, it's you two," he said. "I hope you don't have any earthshaking questions for me."

Gil sat up and wiped his forehead with a thin, ragged handkerchief. He had a book in his lap, *The Journals of Lewis and Clark.*

Henny's eyes were already fixed on the open page. "Wow," he said. "Is this the whole, complete, unabridged version? I've always wanted to read the real thing."

"This is part of it," said Gil. "Volume two. I'm just doing a little research about what Meriwether Lewis and William Clark found when they came here."

This was a signal to Henny to search his photographic memory. "It took the expedition one year, five months, and two days to get this far," he said, squinting. "And then it took them another month to get to the coast. Sacajawea was with them. That was in 1805."

Henny was getting way off the point. "That wasn't so long ago," I said. "I found an artifact that probably goes back 10,000 or 12,000 B.P. Way back when there was no one around to write about it."

B.P. is something I learned at the museum. Gil explained it to Henny and me when he showed us some of his favorite artifacts. B.P. means Before Present. I wanted Gil to know that I had something really rare and important. I wanted him to understand that we were discussing the Great Discovery.

"Everyone wants to be the firstest with the mostest," said Gil. "Whatever did you find, and how do you know it's that old?"

So I told him about the carved stone bowl. Then I told him about the people who came to the island for some peace and quiet and chose the turtle to be their symbol.

"Tarnation," said Gil. "How could you possibly know any of that? Do you even know the exact horizontal level of that bowl in the soil?"

"Well," I said. "I don't exactly know that. It was just there, way below the waterline, sloshing around in a muddy basin."

"I'm glad to hear that you weren't digging," said Gil. "Digging, excavating, all of that is plain illegal. And when you pull something out of the ground, without recording everything in the midden, the scientists holler and scream because they just lost a bunch of valuable information."

I must have looked confused because Henny started a long effort to straighten me out.

"Midden," said Henny, "is camp dirt, refuse, garbage. This park is built on midden. It's what's been tossed aside in a village. Sometimes it can be ten or twelve feet deep if tribes lived there for hundreds of years. Did you see any of that?"

"I don't think I saw any garbage," I said. "Mostly mud and water and a few little green plants growing around."

"You have to know what to look for," said Gil. "First off, you look for deep black soil. Then you look for the shattered rocks."

"They shattered rocks and then threw them in the garbage?" I said. This didn't make a whole lot of sense to me, but it was getting very interesting. I wished my dad had told me some of these things.

"The rocks look like they've been burned," said Gil. "That's because they were heated up in a fire. Sometimes the rocks cracked."

Henny interrupted Gil. "You start to find bits of bone, ashes, charcoal, flint chips. Then you know you've found an ancient campsite. Depending on how many layers of soil you go through to get there, you can get an idea of how old things are."

I decided I'd better get back out there and look for all this stuff. The site was so old that the midden was probably thirty feet deep, at least, and loaded with evidence of the Turtle People.

"Sometimes," said Gil, "the water erodes the bank and exposes a relic. All of the other things that might have given clues about the area have been washed away. Like in your case, I think. Does that bowl have a little message in it that says made in 10,000 B.P.? Is there a little label there that says 'handcrafted by Turtle People'?"

"There are writings on the side. Maybe you can read them."

I had the feeling that Gil wanted more proof than I had at that moment. I tried to explain my theory about the nature of the island and the people who went there. Gil, for once, looked like he was not going to drop off to sleep at any moment. "Interesting," he said. "I've been studying artifacts and reading archaeological journals for years. No one ever mentioned anything like this."

"That's what makes it such a great discovery," I said, getting excited all over again. "It's totally brand-new. It will put my name in the history books, and yours too, if you care to translate. My mother will love it. My dad will come right back to be in on the celebration."

"Oh, my," said Gil. "You're expecting to get quite a bit out of this one discovery. We may have a problem here."

"I know what problems are," I said, feeling a little bit uneasy. "This is not a problem. This discovery is everything. It's more exciting than a petrified rhinoceros. That island will be better known than Atlantis. Now I just need a little help getting that bowl across the Snake River."

Gil looked at Henny. "Is he always like this?" he asked. "Maybe he's been touched by the sun. Someone should throw him in the river and see if he comes to his senses."

"He loves the river," said Henny. "He's in it every day and it hasn't brought him to his senses, yet."

I thanked Henny for his kind support. But it didn't matter what they said. I still had the bowl. It was rare and wonderful and I knew it without a doubt.

"Just explain to me once more where that bowl

is and we'll see if we can't get it," said Gil.

"I buried it," I said. "It's under some tumbleweeds in the middle of the island."

"That's what I thought you said," said Gil. "Now what are you going to do if a windstorm comes up and blows those tumbleweeds way off in another direction? We can't go digging all over that island. It's a big fine and maybe prison if you get caught."

"We were hoping to use your rowboat to bring the bowl back," said Henny. "And soon, before a windstorm comes up."

"That old rowboat is in the lagoon by the bridge, way downstream from the island. Don't you have anything better than that?" said Gil.

"Nope," I said.

"Well," said Gil. "I hope at least one of you has got very strong arms, because there'll be lots of rowing to do. I'm too old for this nonsense. Got no lung power anymore. Think you can handle it?"

Gil had a look in his pale blue eyes that told me he was hooked. He wanted to see the bowl just as much as we did.

"You're coming, right?" said Henny. "We can use the boat?"

"I'm going," said Gil. "If you want something, you've just got to go after it. Otherwise you end up old, with no memories, except of all the things you wish you had done."

So things weren't perfect, but they were moving along. I could hardly wait until we got the bowl, and when we did, Dad was going to get the call of a lifetime.

7

WE PUT OUR BIKES IN GIL'S TRUCK AND GOT IN FOR
a ride to the rowboat.

"Ah," said Henny. "Give us a blast of that air
conditioner."

"What makes you think this truck is air-conditioned?" said Gil. "Wouldn't have it. Just one
more thing that could go wrong."

Lots of things had already gone wrong with this
truck. It had a cracked windshield, lots of body
dents and rust, and ripped seats. But it did do
something right. It started.

"We've got to hurry," I said. "I have to be home by five-thirty."

"Well, that's very interesting," said Gil. "Imagine how far Captain Lewis would have gotten if his mother said, 'Now, Meriwether, be sure to be home for supper.' "

"My mom makes a lot of rules," I said. "I'm in a lot of trouble if I don't follow them."

"We'll be lucky to get home before dark," said Henny. "It's a long way to that island when you have to go upstream."

I hoped Mom would understand. Dad would, for sure. He'd take me to the island if he knew. He probably would take me to the Burke Museum in Seattle to consult an expert, if he knew. He would buy me dinner in a restaurant and toast my success with a root-beer float, if he knew.

I'd called Dad at Uncle Doug's in Seattle three times. Three times I got that answering machine. And he didn't call back. But he wouldn't be able to ignore me if I left a message that really grabbed his attention.

Or maybe he could read about my Great Discovery in the papers. Then he would know that there are important things going on in my life.

We went back to the highway, crossed the bridge again, and went down to the lagoon. Right away I saw the boat that had to belong to Gil. It was an old wooden thing, with little touches of green where it might have been painted once. The oarlocks were loose and rusty. And the oars were cracked.

But that was just the beginning.

"There's water in the bottom," said Henny. "This boat has a leak."

"It's nothing," said Gil. "Just some seepage. Hop in and I'll get the rope."

"There are no life jackets, no fire extinguisher, no sonar, no compass," said Henny. "Does the Coast Guard know about this boat?"

"I hardly use it anymore, for Pete's sake," said Gil. "And we don't need those things. Just follow the river."

"There are laws," said Henny. "There are laws about going out in boats like this."

"Those laws are for big boats, with motors," said Gil. "This isn't the *Queen Mary.* Besides, I'm retired, remember? Takes a lot of money and work to keep an old wooden boat in shape."

"When it comes to artifacts," said Henny, "you do everything by the book. Just what is the difference here? The Coast Guard must think you can't read."

"This boat and I are from another era," said Gil. "We keep going on common sense and memories.

Maybe we're short on common sense, but gosh, do we have a lot of memories."

I could see that Henny needed something more than memories to ease his mind. "Really, Gil," I said. "Don't you have anything to put into this boat?"

"Dagnabit," said Gil, leaning over to look under the seats. "I guess those things are up in the truck. I'll be right back."

Henny started pacing up and down on the dock.

"What do we really know about this guy?" he whispered as soon as Gil was gone. "Maybe the truck and boat are falling apart because Gil is out of money. Maybe he's going to take the bowl and leave us on the island."

"C'mon, Henny," I said. "You're afraid of the water, that's all. There's no reason to be paranoid about Gil."

"Suddenly you're an instant judge of character," said Henny. "What do you know about people? You spend all your time avoiding them."

"Henny, last time I tried to get you too close to the water, you were sure the guy with the big inboard cruiser wanted to run you over. And what happened?"

"Well, he sat on the beach and ate hot dogs all day. But he was probably thinking about it, and if he ever took the boat out . . ."

Then Gil was back and I gave Henny a reassuring smile.

"Well, are we going or not?" said Gil. He got into the front of the boat and looked up at us. He had *The Journals of Lewis and Clark* with him, and two cushions. It looked like I wouldn't get one.

"We're going," I said, and got into the middle by the oars. "Come on, Henny," I said. "Get in. Put your foot in the middle of the boat so you won't tip it."

Henny swallowed hard. "You mean this boat might tip?" he said.

"Listen, young fellow," said Gil. "I've been out in this boat hundreds of times. It won't tip."

Henny put one foot in and Gil let go of the rope. Henny no longer had a choice. It was either get all the way in or fall into the river.

Henny got in. He even managed to move toward the back and sit down.

I gave Henny a grateful look. "Relax," I said. "Take it all in. Remember *everything.*"

I assumed reporters and biographers would want lots of specific information when they wrote about the Great Expedition. The details would make good reading. The hot sun beating on our heads, the leaky boat, the lack of good supplies. The setup was perfect.

Dad always said you couldn't do a job correctly without the proper tools. Well, I was going to do it with a whole boatload of improper equipment. He would be doubly amazed.

I started to row out of the lagoon.

GIL HANDED HENNY ONE OF THE CUSHIONS AND A one-pound coffee can from under the seat. Henny was very suspicious.

"What's this for?" he asked. "Why are you giving me this stuff?"

"The cushion is for your sitter," Gil said, "and the can is for the water."

"What water?" said Henny. He didn't look too good.

"Well, there's bound to be a little extra water with the three of us sitting here," said Gil. "And your friend hasn't done much rowing. He splashes quite a bit over the side."

Henny glared at me. "Quit it," he said. "Just quit splashing water into the boat."

I tried to be smooth. By the time we got out into the river, I was doing better.

"Two steps forward, one step backward," said Gil. "We aren't making much progress against this current."

"I'll go out a little farther," I said. "Maybe the current won't be so strong out there."

I felt very good about things. My rowing was getting better. We were closer to the bowl. The crew was busy and in high spirits.

Gil was reading from *The Journals of Lewis and Clark*. Henny was searching his photographic memory for loose information.

"Says here that one time, the expedition had nothing to eat but bear fat and candles," said Gil. "Now that's real interesting."

Henny sighed. "Sometimes they ate buffalo humps, and wolf meat, and a root called Wappato. Wappato is supposed to taste like potatoes. Boy, am I hungry. Did anybody bring a snack?"

"There might be a few crackers under your seat," said Gil. "Then again, there might not be."

"There is a box of Wheat Thins," said Henny

after he rummaged around under the seat. "It is soggy, dirty, crushed, and unfit for human consumption."

"I never eat them," said Gil. "I feed them to the kingfishers. But if you're really hungry, they're better than candles."

Henny waved the box in the air. "Is anything going to go right on this trip?" he said. A sea gull swooped down and almost got the box.

The crew was starting to feel the hardships. Desperation and hunger had set in. I figured the people from my island would look to the turtle for an answer to this situation, so I tried to do the same.

The only thing I could come up with was that the armor on a turtle was much better protection than an old rowboat. Did this mean we should have waited for something with a sleeker, stronger, fiberglass hull? I decided not to say anything about this to Henny.

"Two steps forward, two steps backward," said Gil. "The current is worse out here. We are not getting *anywhere.*"

"Just give me a little time," I said. I thought of a turtle out of water, slow, plodding, finally getting somewhere, but not very fast. "We'll get there eventually," I added. "Slow, but sure."

Henny bailed out a few tablespoons of water.

"We might sink first," he said. "We should go back."

"Hang on to your cushion," said Gil. "That should give you a sense of security."

Henny grabbed the cushion and held it out for us to examine. "Look at this thing," he said. "Cracked, split, stained, torn, with a little fishhook on the handle. Here's a label. Maybe it has directions." Henny gasped. *"Do not use this as a flotation device,"* he read aloud. "Why can't I use this as a flotation device? You said I could use it." Henny's voice squeaked.

"You can use it," said Gil. "I'm telling you, you can use it."

"Well, now," said Henny. "That is simply a great relief. You have just taken a great worry from me. Sure I can use it. But will it hold me up?"

Gil picked up his book and started to read. "Did you know that everyone wanted to trade Lewis and Clark for blue beads?" he said. "Have you ever found any blue beads?"

"You're trying to change the subject," said Henny. "I want to know if this cushion will hold me up."

The tone of this conversation started to make me uncomfortable. It reminded me of my parents trying to talk about the farm and things. I wanted to take a swim, but I didn't. I just kept pulling the oars back and forth, back and forth.

Suddenly there was a loud snap. I lost my balance and fell back onto Gil.

"What are you doing?" said Gil. "Don't stop rowing or we will lose our position."

"Yeah," said Henny. "Don't stop rowing. *Don't stop rowing!*"

"Something happened," I said. "Did you hear that snap?"

Gil saw it first. "Well, there's your trouble. That doohickey is broke, there."

The right oar went straight out like it was supposed to, and then bent down into the water like it wasn't supposed to. Like a broken wing.

"Omigosh, what're we gonna do?" I said. "Now we can't row at all."

Henny put his arms through the cushion straps and glared at me. His eyes said that I had gotten them into this mess, and could I please have the courtesy to fix things up. What did he think? That I had a 100-horsepower motor hidden in my pocket? Or that I knew the whereabouts of a 300-pound armored reptile who could pull us to shore?

Well, I couldn't do anything. The only place we were going was downstream. "No steps forward, five steps backward," said Gil. "Dingbustit. I wanted to see that bowl."

For a while, nobody said anything. Not even Henny.

I watched all the details of the expedition go by in reverse and wondered how the Turtle People would answer this one. Well, a turtle would plunge into the water and swim away. What kind of answer was that? I could do it, but what about Henny and Gil? It would be hard to live your whole life based on a turtle. What about times like this, when you needed to think about other people?

We went under the bridge and past the lagoon.

I thought about my mother, who seemed to be leaving the family, bit by bit, and not thinking about anybody else. I felt like she was ready to plunge into the water, ready to swim away. But it didn't make any sense. Dad was the one who was gone. And she was here, sort of.

I figured I must be missing something. You probably had to study turtles in depth, in detail, for years and years, before they could show you the answer.

I didn't have the time. Already my hopes and ambitions were vanishing into the hot summer sky. The bowl was up and we were going down. Definitely the wrong direction.

Gil finally broke the silence. "If I'd known we'd

be adrift like this," he said, "I'd have brought my pole. Look at the salmon down there."

"What would we do with them?" said Henny. "I suppose we'd have to eat them raw."

"Raw! We don't eat salmon raw in these parts. You cook 'em up when you get home."

"How are we going to get home?" said Henny. "Right now we are going under the railway trestle, which you could see if you'd quit looking at those fish."

"I'll try to steer us over to the side," I said. Actually I had been trying to do that for a while, but was getting nowhere.

I gave it another try, but finally had to give it up. The boat seemed to have a mind of its own. But it didn't seem to know that a boat without a rower could be headed for disaster.

Henny suddenly sat up and fluttered his hand in front of my face. "Look at this," he said. "The water's all churned up. Look at the whirlpools and eddies." Water slapped the side of the boat and splashed over the top. Henny bailed it out before it had time to puddle.

The boat started to turn to the right, then the left, then right again. The water was rough and swirled us around.

"Great," said Henny. "We are headed out into the main current of the Columbia River. We are on

our way to McNary Dam, with fourteen genera-
tors and a hundred-and-eighty-three-foot drop. If
we end up in the blades of a turbine, we might
generate enough electricity for a few one-hun-
dred-watt light bulbs." Henny whistled and wiped
his brow. "Too bad you don't have your braces
yet, Richie. An electric charge builds up in wire."

Henny bailed out more water and then took off
his shirt to sop up a little moisture in the corner.
Gil shouted to some people in the park. No re-
sponse.

I tried to steer us again, but the two rivers
bumped into each other and the currents were too
strong for me.

"Relax," said Gil. "A boat is coming toward us.
We can get a tow."

"That's some boat," said Henny. "Shiny and
clean. And look. It has sonar and radar and life
rings. We're saved!"

It was a Coast Guard boat. They checked to see
what we had and what we didn't have in the way
of equipment.

"Looks like an expedition to rediscover the
Pacific Ocean," said the man in the bow. "Only in
this century, you have to take along certain safety
devices." He checked something off on his clip-
board.

"Yeah," said another. "And this *Journal of Lewis and Clark* could use an update. I bet they don't mention any of the four dams you visit if you keep heading downstream."

They wrote out a ticket, and Gil scrunched it up and stuffed it in his pocket. I wondered what it said but wasn't sure if I should be paying much attention to these details. Would a reporter *insist* on writing about this part?

The Coast Guard towed us back to the lagoon. Nobody said much, but Henny did put his shirt back on. It was wet, dirty, and covered with Wheat Thins crumbs.

We'd had a real setback, and everybody was down. We didn't get the bowl, and we didn't check the midden.

Worst of all, I didn't have anything to call Dad about, not yet.

On the other hand . . . we'd avoided McNary Dam and we didn't sink.

And best of all, we had just enough energy to come up with a real solution: *Plan B.*

GIL DROPPED US OFF AT HENNY'S. THE SKY WAS AL-
ready pink, pink, pink, and orange. All that dust
up there makes terrific sunsets.

Except that sunsets come so late in the day.
After the "dinner hour," long after that.

I jumped out and pulled my bike off the truck.
In a flash, I was on it and heading for home.

"That is daredevil, reckless speed," Henny
called after me. "You're already late. You can't
fix it."

"Don't worry about me," I yelled back. "Put
everything you've got into Plan B."

I just kept pushing those pedals around, faster

59

and faster. I pedaled the way I swim, until my throat ached and my lungs pulled. I raced along until I was breathless.

That's how I felt—breathless, sitting on the edge, waiting to see which way things would fall.

Mom would be mad, but how mad? A windstorm would come soon, but how soon? Someday Dad might blow in, but when?

I had to get that bowl back, and then things would fall into place. I just needed to come up with my part of Plan B.

Plan B was probably not good scientific method, like the great archaeologists would use. It was a plan to come up with a plan. It was loose and wide open. It was the kind of plan that needs a touch of genius to finish it off.

Each of us was supposed to think of something—something good. Then early in the morning, we'd mix 'em and match 'em and blend the ideas together. Soon after that, the bowl would be back in my hands.

I didn't have an idea yet, but something would come to me. After all, I am a night person, just like my dad. Great thoughts often come to me late, very late. The only problem is they come in bits and pieces and it takes forever.

I tried to get some piece of an idea started before I got home, but then there I was and Blue-

boy came running down the driveway. He jumped
up on my bike and almost knocked me over.

"Down," I said. "Down, Blueboy." But he was
on his hind feet, barking and going around in cir-
cles. At least he seemed glad to see me.

Then Ellen showed up. "Where have you
been?" she said. "You missed dinner. Mom is
so-o-o-o mad."

"Maybe she's worried about me," I said. "I'm all
right." I threw a raggedy tennis ball across the
yard and Blueboy took off after it.

"Mom is just plain mad," said Ellen. "She hasn't
said a word for ages. And she got a letter today.
It was from Dad."

"A letter?" I said. "What about the letter? Did
you see it?"

Boy, was I excited. Maybe Dad had figured out
that you couldn't just take off and not talk to anybody. He'd been acting like a turtle out on an
island.

Ellen shook her head. "Mom took it right to her
room. Do you think Dad is coming back?"

"I'm going to get him back, myself. Tomorrow,"
I said.

"What are you doing, Richie? Why are you so
late?"

Before I could answer, Mom came out on the
porch. Her hands were clenched up under her chin

and she looked worried. "Oh, Richie," she said. "You're all right. I thought something must have happened to you."

"Lots has happened to me," I said. "All kinds of things. But what about Dad? What did he say in the letter?"

Mom put her hands down into her pockets. "The sunset looks pretty on the hills over there."

"Mom," I said. "I really want to know."

"He's going to pay us a visit," she said. "Soon." She didn't look happy about it at all. She turned around quickly and walked back into the house.

Boy, was she slipping. She didn't even ground me. She just pulled back into her shell, like a Turtle Person, all right. She was never going to solve anything that way. Maybe that's why the Turtle People died out.

I remembered when Mom used to sit on the porch in Seattle, watching Ellen and me play. Sometimes she would sing one of the old songs about streamlets and meanderings and Dad would try some harmony and sing very low. Then they'd both laugh.

I didn't think that would ever happen again. It had been a long time ago. Ellen was so little, she probably didn't remember Mom that way. I wished I knew the words. Someone needed to sing them to Ellen.

Ellen came up and sat down on the steps. "You're not supposed to miss dinner," she said.

"Dinner, sminner," I said. "Some things are more important than meat loaf and green beans."

"Like what? Nobody ever tells me what's going on."

"Why don't you go play with Blueboy, Ellen. I've got some heavy thinking to do."

"You, Richie, are a total pest and you don't even know it." She picked up a chewed-up Frisbee and tossed it out to Blueboy.

I went in and called Dad's number in Seattle. I couldn't believe I got the machine, *again.* I'd already left four messages on that machine and that was enough. Wherever Dad's island was, he was out of reach.

I wanted Mom to tell me more about the letter. I went through the kitchen to find her and there was another momo. THE CHEF HAS GONE TO BED. SERVE YOURSELF. MOM.

It was one note too many. I went up to my room and made a sign of my own.

KEEP OUT!

This means you!

Burglars
Treasure Hunters

Archaeologists
Swimming Pool Designers
Vacuum Salesmen
Missing Persons
Women
Children
Sinking Ships

If you can read this sign,
you are too close to my room.

GET BACK!

I put the sign on my door and closed it with a loud bang. Then I plopped down on the bed. My arms ached. My legs ached. My head ached. I was so tired and disappointed, I wasn't even hungry.

I stared at the stripes in the wallpaper and tried to think of Plan B, but my eyelids drooped. I looked over at my collection of Oz books and then plopped into the beanbag chair, but it didn't help. My brain was like an empty billboard that read THIS SPACE FOR RENT.

For a night person, I wasn't doing so well. I was practically asleep. I just lay there, like a turtle, waiting for someone to put me up on the fence. I read that once: If you ever see a turtle up on a fence, you know he had to have help.

Maybe I needed some help. I opened up my old *Animal Encyclopedia* to the *T* section and then drew a box turtle and a snapping turtle. Snap. Snap. That didn't solve anything. The problem was that our family had fallen apart and nobody was talking about it.

I thought it would be nice to have an answering machine that could really answer questions. I thought it would be nice to have my bowl sitting on the desk in my room, with Mom and Dad and Ellen there to see it.

I thought it would really be nice if someone would make me a plate of teeny grape sandwiches. That's what Dad used to do. Cut the grapes in half and put cheese in the middle.

But all of this had nothing to do with Plan B. I tried to concentrate on Plan B.

And then I fell asleep.

When I woke up, it was early morning and someone was pounding on the door, hard.

"What's this sign on your door?" said Ellen. "I can't read all those big words."

"You can read *keep out!*" I said. "That's the only part that matters."

I heard Ellen slump against the door. "Nobody wants to talk to me anymore," she said. "I miss everybody, all the time. I want to know what you've been doing. I want to know where Dad is. I want Mom to play with me."

I opened the door and Ellen fell into the room with a big pout on her face. "Come on in," I said. "You can talk to me. I'll tell you about my plan."

"Oh, goody," said Ellen, and she started to perk up. "A plan. I just love plans. Is that anything like homework?"

Ellen had been waiting her whole life to get some homework. She hadn't gotten any yet in school.

"This is better than homework," I said, and I told her about the bowl, and Gil, and the rowboat. I even told her about the Coast Guard.

"Boy," she said. "Are you going to be in trouble when Mom finds out."

"She's not going to find out, is she, Ellen?" I said. "Wait until I get the bowl back. Wait until I'm rich and famous and everyone wants to know how I did it. Then she won't mind about the details."

"I have to get some paper and a pencil," said Ellen. "Then I'll make you a plan."

"There's some on my desk," I said. "We've got to hurry. I should be on my way already."

Ellen drew a picture of a helicopter landing on

an island. I sighed. I couldn't think of anything good either.

Ellen drew a picture of a submarine, and a robot, and a man with a basket on top of his head. I shook my head. "None of those will do," I said. "Sorry."

"This plan is hard work," said Ellen. "Why did you draw these turtles in the back of the notebook?"

"Well," I said, "I thought you could get all the answers from a turtle."

"That's silly, Richie. Turtles don't even talk."

"Yeah. Let's get something to eat. Is Mom up yet?"

"She's in her room with the door closed," said Ellen. "I'll pick out the cereal."

Ellen ran downstairs and I got dressed. Then I went down to the kitchen and padded across the clean, shiny floor to the counter. I sat over my bowl of cereal, and thought, and thought some more. Nothing. A big zero. It was awful. I was desperate for a good idea.

I heard a door open and my mother shuffle down the hallway. And then I heard the vacuum roaring in the room that Dad used for an office.

"Are you crying?" said Ellen. "Are those tears in your eyes?"

"That's allergies," I said. "I wish Mom wouldn't scrub out this kitchen with bleach all the time."

"Well, I'm glad you're not crying," said Ellen. "Dad will come back sometime, you know. And I don't really think you're a pest."

"Well, you should, because I am one, definitely."

I watched the little pieces of puffed corn float across the milk and I thought about floating and Indians and suddenly I had my plan.

"I've got it," I said.

"That's not fair," said Ellen. "I wanted to make the plan."

"That's the good part. You can help. I just need to borrow one little thing from you and I'm out the door."

"You can't borrow my princess robe," said Ellen. "You can't borrow anything that would get ruined in the water."

"Don't worry," I said. "What I'm going to borrow was made for the water. It was made for this plan. If this was homework, we would get an *A plus*."

I WAS THE LAST ONE TO GET TO THE MEETING SPOT.
Gil and Henny looked worried.

"We weren't sure that this was the right place,"
said Gil. "I was just about to drive us up to the
next island."

"This is it," I said. "Can't you feel it? Lewis and
Clark came right by here. The Turtle People, or
some ancient people, came right by here too, and
now it's our turn. We are going to bring in the
archaeological find of the century."

Gil shook his head. "Why didn't you bring a

trumpet?" he said. "And a few flags. Then we could do this in real style."

What a great idea, I thought. But it was too late for that. "Our first job is to get the bowl," I said. "What did you bring for Plan B?"

"I brought the seat cushions," said Gil. "That's the best I could do. You can swim out there and pull the bowl back on the cushion."

"You forgot the rock-and-roll effect," said Henny. "A boat makes a big wave, rocks the cushion, and the bowl rolls off."

"There's always something I don't think of," said Gil. "So what's your idea?"

"Well," said Henny. "I brought my newspaper delivery bag. Richie can swim over with it, put the bowl deep inside, and swim back, just like that."

"Henny," I said, "it is clear that you do not understand much about swimming in this current. You don't understand much about swimming, period."

"I understand," said Henny. "You need both your arms to keep going. That's the beauty of this plan. Your arms will be free. You wear the bag on your shoulders."

"You don't understand drag," I said. "That's like tying a whale to the bottom of a ship. It's like throwing a baseball wrapped in a sweatshirt. It's like rowing a boat with only one oar."

"I get it," said Henny. "So what's your idea? I hope you have one."

I pulled out a square piece of vinyl from under my T-shirt. It was orange and black and brown.

"This is it," I said. "This is the key to Plan B that will make it work."

"Great," said Henny. "What is it? A Halloween bag?"

I grabbed the orange corner and shook out the square. It unfolded into an impressive piece of vinyl about three feet long.

"Ta*da*," I said. When you are about to become a big part of history, you have to do things with a flourish.

"Ta*da,* what?" said Henny. "I still don't get it."

"It's a canoe," I said. "From a modern-day toy store. We're going to do this just the way the Indians would have done it." I could hardly wait to see how this would look in the history books. It was too bad Dad wasn't there. I wanted him to be in the footnotes, at least.

"You're going to paddle over in that little contraption?" said Gil. "Hardly looks big enough."

"It's for the bowl, not me," I said. "The sides are high and puffy. The bowl won't come out. I'll push the canoe in front of me, like a paddleboard. Isn't that a great idea?"

"I know about paddleboards," said Henny.

"You tried to get me to use one at the beach. Paddleboards do not allow for free use of the arms."

"It will work," I said. "The canoe will hold me up while I kick like crazy."

"Sounds like a lot of work to me," said Gil. "You planning to blow it up over here, or over there?"

"I guess I'll blow it up over there," I said. "I wish someone had brought a rope, though. Then you could pull it back and I could follow."

"Well, I brought a rope," said Gil. "But I didn't mention it because it's not long enough. It's a long ways out to that island. Can't imagine how you ever swim there."

"You have to dive in by that sagebrush," I said, pointing upstream. "By the time you swim across, the current takes you right to that sandbar on the end."

"Your parents must be mighty proud of you, being able to swim like that."

"They will be," I said. "Just as soon as I get the bowl back."

"Well, I admire you for doing it. You really know how to go after what you want. You'll have some great memories when you get old."

"Oh, oh," said Henny. "The wind is kicking up. You can see it coming right across the desert. You'd better not go, Richie."

"It'll be all right," I said. "I'm the one who's going, not you." I checked the canoe for holes and cracks. It was in great condition. Ellen just got it for her birthday in June. I folded it up and put it back under my shirt. I tucked the shirt in carefully, all around.

"Take the rope," said Gil. "It might come in handy."

I checked Gil's rope for frayed edges and loose ends. It wasn't too bad, so I tied it around my waist.

"I feel kind of useless," said Henny. "What are we supposed to do?"

"This adventure needs witnesses," I said. "Remember the little things. Record the time, the weather, everything you see."

"Are you going to go?" said Gil. "Or are you waiting for a Coast Guard inspection?"

"I'm just making sure that the gear is in proper order," I said. I wanted this expedition to be different. I had every intention of making it work.

Forget adventure, forget the high drama. It was time to play it smart.

"**Don't go now,**" **said Henny. "The wind is really** starting to blow."

"I'm going," I said.

Gil put his finger in his mouth and then put it up in the air. "Wind's coming from the Saddle Mountains," he said. "It's probably picking up a lot of dust."

Wind. Dust. I was getting a little tired of hardships. If you have too many hardships, you never make it into the history books, period.

But the history books didn't seem so important

anymore. The main thing was to get out to that island, and quick.

"Might be better if you wait," said Gil. "This storm could be a doozie."

"Yeah, don't go now," said Henny.

"I'm *going*," I said. "Before the wind moves my tumbleweeds."

I checked the gear around my waist, and then got into the river.

As I walked out, the wind ruffled up the water. That made it harder to swim. Another darn hardship!

No matter how I swam, the gear was a drag on my body. And no matter how I tried to breathe, splashes of Snake River kept finding my mouth. I choked. I gasped. I gagged. I gargled. Yuck! A bit of that slimy goo taste was in the river.

"Is this fair?" I yelled into the wind. I didn't hear any answer and it took too much energy to yell anything else.

I kept on stroking. Left arm. Right arm. Breathe. Gasp. Choke. It was hard to swim with all that wind whirling around. If you wanted to do any breathing, that is. Left arm. Right arm. Kick. Breathe.

I was so concerned with getting oxygen into my system that I almost missed the sandbar. I started to kick like crazy to get back upstream. That's when I realized that my feet could touch the bottom.

I shuffled through the water and flopped down on the sand like a beached whale. Boy Wonder, in his triumphant return to the island, couldn't even stand up to enjoy it. And it was no fun lying down either, not with the wind blowing sand in my face.

I couldn't imagine that the great explorers did anything that made them look this pathetic, but Henny had told me stories.

Once Clark got treed by a bear and was up there for hours. Lewis got shot in the rear end by one of his men who thought he was an elk. And Lewis carried parts for a boat halfway across the continent and then found out it wouldn't float when he needed it.

But Lewis and Clark were successful because they brought plenty of supplies and planned well. I checked my gear. Everything looked good but there wasn't enough.

I wished there was a blanket because the wind made me cold. Then I wished there were goggles to keep the swirling sand out of my eyes. Lots of Indians had swollen eyes and Clark treated them with a medical solution he carried to bathe the eyes. Too bad he didn't stash some of this "eye water" on the island.

I wished I were home, where all you do is shut the windows. But then what? The house was just too empty.

I didn't know where the Turtle People went when the wind blew, but it didn't matter. I didn't want to go anywhere except right to the bowl.

The wind was becoming a regular storm. A whirlwind blew parts of my island up into the air. For a moment, I couldn't see much of anything except sand. My mouth and ears collected sand. My hair was caked with the stuff.

When the whirlwind danced to another part of the island, I got up to check the midden, to see if I could find any more clues about the bowl. I walked through the waving bunch grass, over to the other side. But there was the river, right back up where it used to be. And the midden was gone from everybody's reach.

Wind, cold, sand, currents, and no midden. Lots of hardships no matter how well you check the gear. The trick was to keep on going, no matter what.

Then, a big tumbleweed rolled past and left scratches on my legs. Another landed on my chest. The tumbleweeds were on the move and my markers for the bowl were gone.

I sat down on the sand and almost cried. The island had always been a familiar rest stop. Now it was a tangled maze without a road sign in sight.

"Henny! Gil," I called out. "What do I do?"

The words blew right back into my mouth. I guessed it was all up to me. I could go back with it or without it, but not until I had made every effort.

The wind eased up a bit and I ran toward the middle of the island. I searched everywhere, but nothing looked right. All the tumbleweeds were gone and now the wind was blowing away the top layers of sand.

So I closed my eyes real tight and pretended it was nighttime, when I do my very best work.

That's when I remembered. A few more looks around and I saw it, a big bump in the swirling dunes. The anthill. How could I forget about it? I could have kissed that anthill.

But I didn't. Instead I started to dig. The ants didn't even bother me. They were probably in some tunnel, out of the storm.

I dug sand out with both hands, in a fury. Then the wind blew some back in. But I was faster. The hole got bigger.

And then, there it was. The Great Discovery, rediscovered!

It felt so good to have it in my hands. It had been up to me to find it, and the job was done!

Finally, at last, something had gone my way.

12

ONCE THINGS START GOING YOUR WAY, IT'S LIKE finally getting your bike to the top of the hill. You huff and puff forever, and then suddenly you're there. It's relaxation and freewheeling all the way down.

I felt good and expected to coast for a while. But nothing else really changed. The wind still howled and sand pelted my body. My eyes were swollen. My nose was plugged. And I was still on the wrong side of the river.

But something new was going on with me. It wasn't that I thought there'd be no more problems.

It's just that they didn't seem so big. I felt like I could handle them, or leave them behind.

Maybe that's how Lewis and Clark felt when they finally reached the Pacific Ocean. They had problems, but they still got things done. Lots of things.

I blew air into the canoe and it puffed right up. No leaks, nothing wrong. Well, there *was* the picture of an eagle on the front. A turtle would have been nice, but maybe I could learn things from a bird, too. Sacajawea means "bird woman." Bet she learned a lot of things from all sorts of animals.

I put the bowl inside and the fit was perfect. There was no space for it to move between the puffy sides.

I wrapped the rope around and around the canoe to make a lid. I didn't want the bowl to fall out if the canoe tipped.

Then I added some rocks to the front end so that the weight would be even.

I checked everything. I thought of every possible thing that could go wrong.

Planning, checking, rechecking. Every expedition needs a leader who takes the time to do things right. Meriwether Lewis, William Clark, Richard Adams Burroughby. Maybe someday everyone would know who I was. But until then, only I knew.

When the canoe went into the water, I hoped that Henny and Gil were getting the details—wherever they were. I couldn't see them. The wind was dying down, but there was still lots of dust in the air.

"Henny, Gil," I yelled. "Mark the time. I'm returning with the bowl."

Nobody answered.

So I started back without any official notation. The history books could refer to it as "the moment of the great dust storm."

The canoe slapped the water and water slapped the canoe. And me. The water was still rough and I gagged some, and choked.

The wind picked up, blowing me in the wrong direction. It took an extra long time to get near the shore. I was way downstream from where I should have been. That's what I discovered when I could finally see far enough to tell.

I heard shouting but couldn't understand the words. Then I saw something swimming toward me. It couldn't be Gil, and it certainly wasn't Henny. I tried to peek over and around the canoe to see.

I hoped it was help. I was really tired. My

legs could hardly kick another kick. My stomach certainly could not take another gulp of the river.

Whatever was coming was dark and shadowy. So I knew it wasn't a sea gull, or a salmon.

Then I heard Henny yelling and screaming. "Here, boy," he said. "Come on back."

And then I saw who it was. Blueboy! Blueboy coming out to retrieve what was in the water. Just like he had been trained to do. Well, almost trained.

"Don't do it," I said. "Blueboy! Do not retrieve this canoe!"

But he did it anyway. Those big canines chomped down on the vinyl boat. All the air that I so successfully put in on the island began to come out. Sssssssssssssssssss.

It sounded like a snake coming out of the Snake River. Sssssssssssss. Ssssssss. The air was coming out fast.

"Grab it, Henny," I said. "Grab the canoe before it sinks."

"I can't reach it yet," Henny said. He looked petrified, with one hand over his stomach, and the other pointed straight out toward the canoe. Then I noticed that his feet were in the water.

"It's going to go-o-o-o-o-o," I screamed. "Grab it!"

Henny splashed in the water up to his thighs. He reached and missed. "Get closer," he yelled. "Get this dog out of the way!"

"It's collapsed. It's sinking!" I said. "Blueboy, *go!*"

Henny got in up to his armpits. "All right," he said. "I got it. I'm going to pull it in."

Henny, *in the Snake River up to his armpits,* held the canoe until I could get a foothold. Then, panting and gasping, we dragged it onto solid ground.

"All right," I said. "It's safe. Thanks, Henny, thanks, thanks, thanks." I could hardly believe it was over. I couldn't believe that Henny was soaking wet.

"It's okay, the fish didn't bite." Henny had a grin on his face and looked pleased about everything. "If I'm going to be a witness, I want to be an involved one. Where did this dog come from, anyway?"

Blueboy pranced and danced on the beach. He jumped over the canoe and around it. He barked and barked.

"Scoot, Blueboy," I said. "We need to take this bowl someplace out of the wind."

Suddenly Blueboy took off up the beach. "Wow," said Henny. "And I thought that dog was untrainable."

"He sees something," I said. "Someone is coming. See the shadow?"

"Hey, Gil," Henny called out. "We got it. Come here and take a look."

Blueboy came running back. He growled hard at the canoe. He sat down on top of it so it wouldn't get away from him.

But it wasn't Gil that Blueboy had gone to meet.

It was someone else.

It was Dad.

13

I WAS SO GLAD TO SEE HIM. DAD LEANED INTO THE wind, big and strong, with his shirtsleeves flapping, and his red hair waving like a flag.

"What's going on here?" he shouted. "Are you all right?"

It was an angry shout. He was angry at *me*. And then I was angry at *him*. I was angry for the whole summer that he left me dangling. I was angry for all the times that I wanted to see him and he wasn't there.

"You, Dad, are a real turtle," I said, and not very

nicely. "You've come too late, too slow. I took care of everything myself."

"What? Took care of what?" he said. "I went to the house and Mom didn't know where you were. Ellen said you'd be here. I brought Blueboy to find you." He looked all around and wrinkled his eyebrows. "You've been in the river? What happened to Ellen's canoe? Who's that old man back there who can hardly breathe in this storm?"

Dad went on and on with lots of questions.

But they weren't the right questions. He never said, "Wow, isn't this amazing? How did you do it?" He never said, "Shall we call the local papers, or take it straight to *Time* magazine?"

He never even said, "Richard Adams Burroughby, you are one stupendous kid. I've sure missed you."

So I stood there in the wind, feeling cold on the outside and colder on the inside. "I've been worried about you, Dad," I said. "And I've been angry. Where have you *been*?"

Dad stared at me for a second, and seemed a little bit confused. "I was fishing with Uncle Doug, up in Alaska," he said. "We kept going out, trying to get one more big catch. You know me . . . once I get started on something."

"How many fish did you need?" I said. "Didn't you ever think about us?"

"I thought about you all the time," he said. "And I just got your messages. Sorry I couldn't answer them sooner. It wasn't right for me to go so far out of reach."

"It was dumb, Dad. It was such a dumb thing to do."

"You're right," he said. "It was absolutely the worst."

Dad coughed and looked down at his shoes. "It's such a windy day to be out here," he said. "Whatever you're doing, it must be very important." Dad came a little closer and rubbed my shivering arms with his big, rough hands. It started to feel like he really *was* back. The old Dad always knew when something was important to me.

"We just finished a great rescue operation," said Henny. He looked around at both of us and decided to continue. "We finally got an Indian bowl back from that island. I've been waiting for forty-three hours and fourteen minutes to see it. I've braved treacherous currents and slippery rocks. I've been subjected to mad dogs and tack weeds and the extreme heat of the desert. . . ."

"We'd better see this thing," Dad interrupted. "Where is it?"

Henny pulled the bowl out of the collapsed canoe. I heard Dad whistle over my shoulder. "Eureka," he said. "You really did find it. *Eureka!*"

Henny examined the bowl, inch by inch, top to bottom.

"It's in mint condition," said Henny. "Not a crack, not a scratch anywhere." He turned the bowl around again. "You're right, Richie," he said. "It was definitely worth a dip in the Snake River."

"Could I hold that for a minute?" said Dad. He hugged it close to his chest and rubbed it with the ends of his fingers. He patted the small turtle head and traced the carvings on the side.

Dad had a big grin on his face. He really liked the bowl, I could see that. He looked over at me and wrapped my shoulders with his big arm. He really liked me too. I could feel it.

He was still the same. Dad still liked the very same things.

"This," said Dad, "is one of the best specimens I've ever seen. Your mom might even like this one. Let's get out of this wind and you can tell me the whole story."

We made our way upstream and found Gil sitting in Dad's car, out of the storm. I showed him the bowl. "Oh, boy," he said and then he coughed. "Ooh, boy, oh, boy, oh boy." Cough. Cough. Cough.

Gil invited us to his house. "In the old days," he

said, "we'd always take a find like this and put it on my table. And then we'd feast our eyes."

"Come on, Blueboy," said Henny. "We're going for a ride." They went with Gil in his truck. Dad and I went in the car.

I told Dad how I found the bowl and I even told him why I went to the island all the time. We took a left turn behind Gil.

Dad told me Mom wanted him to leave for a while and that's how he ended up fishing in Alaska. "Mom knew where I was," he said. "Didn't she tell you?"

"Mom never told us anything," I said. "When she's mad about something, you know she doesn't talk much. Mostly she's been leaving us notes." We followed Gil across the highway, to a side road.

"I guess I should know that," said Dad. "I'll just have to make sure that I tell you things myself."

"Does that mean you're back to stay?" I said. I hoped!

"I'm here to be with you and Ellen," he said, "and to straighten things out on the farm. I earned enough in Alaska to make up for most of the mistakes I made with the pears."

"I'm glad you're back," I said. "And it's not your fault the weather wasn't right."

"It wasn't all the weather," said Dad. "I should have paid more attention to pruning and irrigation. Your mom had the best ideas about that. If you really want to do something, it pays to learn how to do it right."

"Mom didn't seem very happy that you were coming back," I said. "How come?"

Dad didn't answer. He looked straight ahead at the road. I wanted him to look at me. I wanted to see his eyes.

"Mom is still mad," I said. "You're trying to fix things up. What else can you do?"

"I can't do anything," he said, and he leaned up closer to the steering wheel. "Your mother doesn't want to live here anymore. She doesn't want to live with me anymore."

"What do you mean? Where is Mom going?" I was getting grumpy and a little bit scared. I knew Mom had been moving away from us. But I never expected her to get so far that she wouldn't come back.

And what was going to happen to me? That's something else I really wanted to know.

"Mom's going back to Seattle," he said. "She has her old friends there. She might go back to school."

"First you go to Seattle. Now Mom is going. When are you going to get together?"

"We are not getting together," said Dad. "We are just too far apart."

I started to sniff a little bit, and it wasn't allergies. I felt terrible. I rolled a straw back and forth on the floor mat, but it didn't help. I sniffed some more.

"What about . . . what about me, and Ellen?" I said. "Our friends are here. I like the river, and the heat, and the artifacts all over the place. And I like pears, Dad, almost as much as grape sandwiches."

Dad gave a half smile. "That's why we're going to stay," he said. "You and me and Ellen. We're going to try it again. And you can visit Mom as soon as she finds a place to live."

"I thought when you came back, we'd all be together. That's the way you're supposed to fix a problem." I sniffed again and my eyes filled up with tears.

Dad gave me his handkerchief. I wiped my nose and stared out the side window. Lots of tumbleweeds were blowing across the desert and up by the car. "Watch out, Dad," I warned. "Those weeds are going to cross the road!"

"It's all right," said Dad. "Everything will end up all right."

And I knew he wasn't just talking about the tumbleweeds, which blew right past us. "At least,

I know what's going on," I said. "All summer I didn't know."

"I'm sorry," said Dad. "None of this happened very smoothly."

"That's for sure," I said. I watched the tumbleweeds again.

"Things are going to be better," said Dad. "I have a whole new way of looking at the farm. Numbers. If we can grow five thousand pears, we can get ten thousand. I'm prepared for anything. On the boat, I read books and market reports. I wrote away for information from the Farm Bureau. I even found a market for those little teeny pears we get in the back five acres."

"C'mon, Dad, who would want those things?"

"Minnesota," he said. "I guess everybody loves them in Minnesota."

Dad laughed and I laughed. It was the best laugh I'd had all summer.

Then we stopped on a side street, behind Gil's truck. "We're here," said Dad. "What happens now?"

"Gil is going to tell me about the bowl."

We got out and Dad spent about five minutes trying to put Blueboy in the car. "I'm sure Gil doesn't need this monster jumping all over his house. Someday, we're actually going to train him. There must be a good book on the subject."

"Ask Henny," I said. "He could find a book on anything."

Inside, Gil put the turtle bowl in the middle of the table and then showed us a whole freezer full of ice cream. "Just take your pick," he said. "I made it myself. Got one of those new electric ice cream makers from my sister."

The freezer was old and full of frost, but the ice cream was terrific. We sat around the table and tried Red Haven Peach, Yakima Valley Bing, and Eureka Concord. Here we were: Dad, my friend Henny, Gil, and me. The bowl had brought some things together, but not everything.

We licked our spoons and waited for Gil to say something.

He was very quiet.

I took a long look around the room. Henny was sitting on the edge of his chair, Dad was leaning on his elbows, and Gil was taking too much time to get started. All my ideas about the bowl were beginning to melt, just like the last bits of ice cream.

"You haven't told me how old it is," I finally said.

"I wish there were more clues," said Gil. "It looks something like an effigy bowl from two thousand, three thousand years ago. But it's different from the others. I really can't tell for sure."

"Wow, that's a long time ago," said Henny. "I'll have to see if there isn't some way to protect baseball cards for that long."

"You haven't told me what the lines say on the side," I said.

"They're very unusual," said Gil. "They might be a story or a picture, or something we can't even imagine. Sorry that I'm not more help."

"That's okay," I said. "You can't tell me what you don't see."

And I knew I'd been thinking about something that wasn't. Richie, the dreamer, at it again. There weren't any Turtle People. They hadn't written any secret messages on the side of my bowl. And I didn't even miss them. You can't go around acting like turtles all the time. They just don't have all the answers.

"What *do* you know?" said Henny. "What do you know about this bowl?"

Gil rubbed his chin and gazed out the window. "Well," he said. "I know that this is a wonderful, unusual bowl made by a great craftsman, long, long ago."

"We already know that," said Henny. "Now we need some facts, some final bits of historical data before we present this to the museum board."

"There's just one thing, then," said Gil, "before you go."

"What's that?" I said. "We need all the information that we can get."

"Well, I hate to be the one to tell you this," said Gil. "But that ain't necessarily a turtle."

14

THE WINDSTORM BROUGHT IN NEW WEATHER, cooler weather for a change. It started to feel like it was almost time to go back to school.

Henny was totally exhausted for two days. I stayed home and Ellen and I helped Mom pack for Seattle. "I'll write you letters," Mom said. "I'll write often."

I asked her to write me *real* letters. I can figure out when to make ice cubes myself. She said she would.

Before she left, Mom bought a patch kit at the hardware store for Ellen's canoe. I took every-

thing outside because the glue smelled awful.
Then I started to cut out pieces of vinyl to cover
up Blueboy's teeth marks.

Ellen folded her arms in disgust and watched.
"Boy," she said. "I'm not ever lending you anything again."

I always use too much glue, so I asked Mom to
do that part.

"Glad to help," she said. "I haven't helped you
two in a long, long time. I wanted to, but I just
couldn't do anything."

Ellen and I looked at each other. "You did a lot
of some things," said Ellen. "Like vacuuming."

"I did too much of that," said Mom. "And I don't
even like to vacuum. But this, being outside with
you kids. I almost forgot how much fun it can be."

"You're having fun?" said Ellen. "Look at Blueboy. He's jumping all over everything."

Mom laughed and let Blueboy lick her face.

"I'll help too," said Ellen. "I'll keep Blueboy out
of your way." She ran out to the garden shed, and
Blueboy went with her.

"Remember that gray ship model you used to
work on?" said Mom. "Did you ever finish it?"

"Nope," I said.

"How come?" said Mom.

"Because you would never let me leave it out
anywhere."

"I was afraid you'd say that," said Mom. "When you come to visit, you can bring it. I'll make a place where you can keep it out until you're sixty-five, if you want."

"Really?"

"Really," said Mom.

I gave her a hug. And when she left that afternoon, it didn't make much sense, but I felt like things were headed in a better direction. She was going away from us, but in another way, she was also coming back.

Then Dad took Henny and me over to the museum to see what we could find out about the bowl.

Several people looked at it with a deep sigh of admiration. But nobody could tell me anything, exactly.

It wasn't really a turtle bowl because it had tail feathers. It wasn't really a bird bowl because it had four legs and the head of a turtle.

Classification: somewhat similar to zoomorphic specimens No. 27C, 14, & 152, wrote the man at the museum.

It was probably from a time between 4,000 B.P. and 1,500 B.P. Definitely not 12,000 B.P.

Age: unable to document, wrote the man at the museum.

It was most likely made by Stone Age people who came to catch salmon and then left again. But exactly who? Well, there was still that little problem of no midden.

Origin: unknown, wrote the man at the museum.

"You mean there are no answers?" said Henny. "There have to be answers."

Henny gets very flustered when he has nothing to file into his memory bank.

"I would like to study this," said the man at the museum. "It is a piece that demands research. I hope you will let us display it here."

"In a while," I said. "First, I want to hold it, keep it in my room."

"Then we'll take a picture," he said. He picked up a Polaroid from the file cabinet and put a ruler down next to the bowl. He took a shot from the top and one from each side. Then he took a picture of me! I tried to look very dignified, but Henny made me laugh.

"What's the ruler for?" said Henny.

"That's to give us an indication of the size," said the man at the museum. "We'll keep this in our file with all the necessary information. Be sure to check back with us. There are several digs going on through the university. Perhaps something will turn up like your bowl, but under better circumstances."

"I want answers," said Henny as we left the museum. "I'll be back for answers. Maybe we could even go on a dig."

"I'll take you on a real dig," said Dad. "A university-supervised project, and we'll learn to do it right."

"This is turning out better than I thought," I said. "In fact, everything is very good." I had a big smile on my face.

Henny gave me a look like I had been out in the sun too long. "It's not the firstest with the mostest," he said. "It's not even a turtle."

"That's what makes it so great," I said. "It's like a strange green light flashing in the sky. It's like a twenty-five-inch footprint in your backyard. It's a mystery."

I held the bowl up high so everyone could get one more good look. "Here it is," I said. "A great archaeological mystery of the lower Snake River."

"Hey, that's pretty good," said Henny. "How come I never thought of that?"

"Because Richie's the dreamer," said Dad. "And you're the guy with all the facts."

"It's not that simple," I said.

"Yeah," said Henny. "We're all dreamers-thinkers-doers."

"And today," I said. "I even feel a little bit famous."

Brenda Z. Guiberson:

BECOMING A WRITER WAS NOT ON MY MIND AS A child. I had five sisters and two brothers, and for a while, three foster children in the family. We never sat around much and were usually out along the Columbia River, which ran past our backyard in Richland, Washington.

In high school and college, I took many science classes and was a little surprised to finally end up with degrees in fine art and English. Along the way, I tried out several things; copywriter, wood and stained-glass worker, letter carrier.

The idea of creating children's books started with my son, Jason. He used to bring home dozens of books from the library and ask to hear them over and over again. We were having a very good time and it sank in. After years in this training ground, I finally got up the courage to write. Now I don't want to stop.

I live near Seattle with my husband and son, a workhorse of a computer, and a closet full of art supplies for those days when pictures seem better than words.